This Little Tiger book
belongs to:

_____

_____

_____

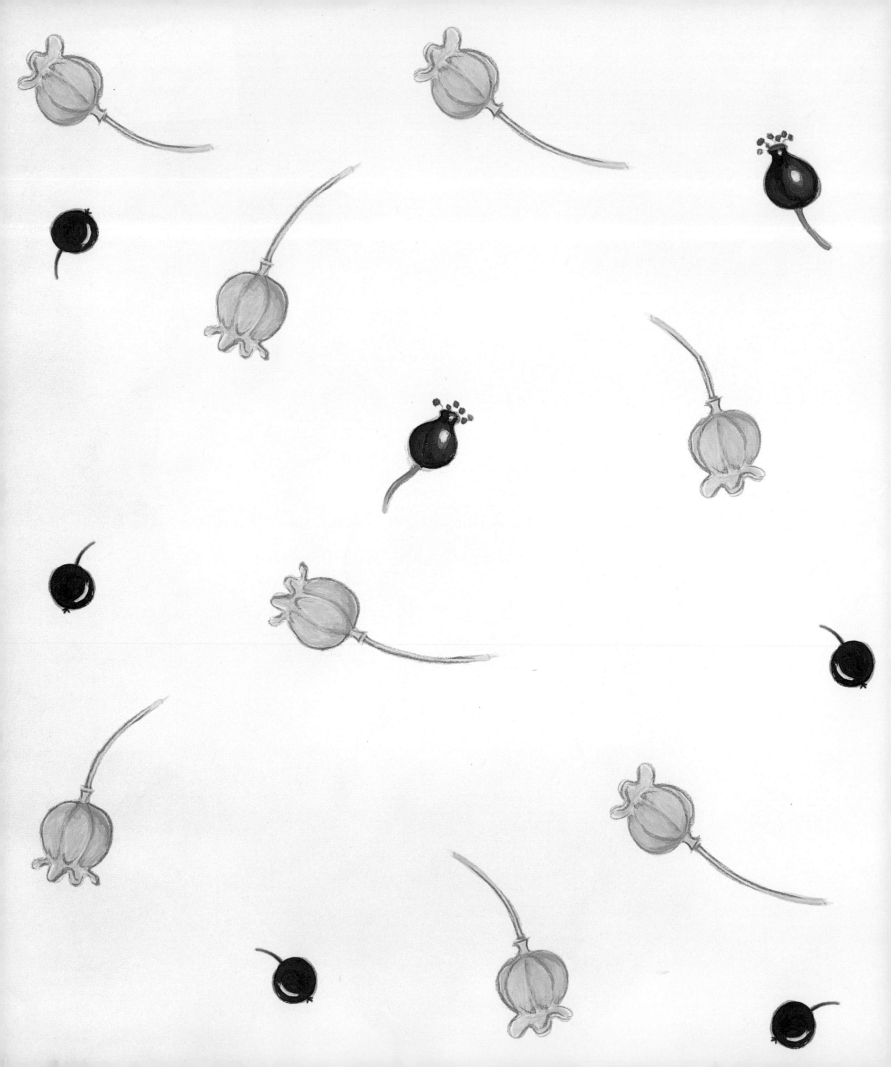

For Olivia, Suzanne, and John Keane
~ S M

For Norie – for all your hard work
in the background!
~ A E

LITTLE TIGER PRESS
1 The Coda Centre,
189 Munster Road, London SW6 6AW
www.littletiger.co.uk

First published in Great Britain 2015
This edition published 2015

Text copyright © Steve Metzger 2015
Illustrations copyright © Alison Edgson 2015

Steve Metzger and Alison Edgson have asserted
their rights to be identified as the author and illustrator of this
work under the Copyright, Designs and Patents Act, 1988

A CIP catalogue record for this book is available from the British Library

Printed in China · LTP/1400/1155/0615

2 4 6 8 10 9 7 5 3 1

Waiting for Santa

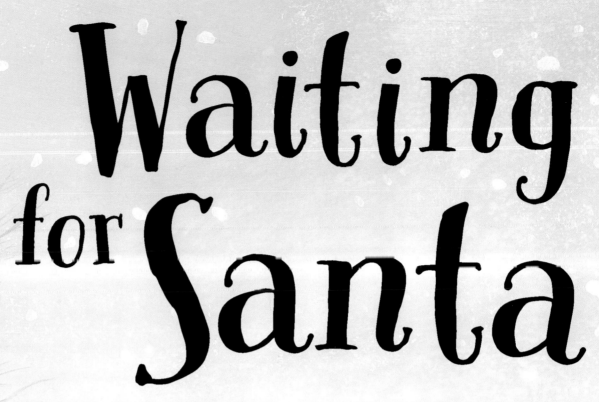

Steve Metzger · Alison Edgson

LITTLE TIGER PRESS
London

Bear woke early with a tingle in his tummy.
"Wake up, everybody!" he called. "Tomorrow's
Christmas! We've got to get ready for Santa Claus!"

"Santa's not coming!" Badger grumbled.
"He doesn't even know we're here!"

"He'll come!" Bear cried. "We just have to believe!"
    "What's all the fuss?" asked Mole. "Is Santa
really coming?"
    "Will there be presents?" squeaked Mouse.
    "Stop this nonsense!" Badger said.
"Santa's not coming – this year . . .
or *any* year!"

But Bear was hopping with excitement.
"Santa will come!" he cheered. "He just
needs some help to find us."

Bear's forest friends talked it over.
   "Maybe he's right," said Hedgehog.
   "Why don't we give it a try?" said
Mole and Mouse together.
   "If we must!" huffed Badger.

All day long, the friends were busy,
busy, busy.

"Santa will love our sign," Mole
said, "if he's here to read it."

"He'll be here!" Bear smiled.

"Santa's reindeer will love these snacks," Mouse said, "if they're here to eat them."

"They'll be here!" Bear declared.

"Santa will love our Christmas tree," Hedgehog said, "if he's here to see it."

"He'll be here! We just have to believe!" Bear exclaimed. And he dashed off into the woods.

"Where's Bear off to now?" Mole asked.
"Maybe he's given up and gone home,"
Badger grumped. "Like *we* should!"

But Bear was back in an instant.

"Look at my Christmas star!" he cheered.
"I hope Santa will like it."

"But our tree is enormous!" Mole said.
"How ever will we reach the top?"

"We'll do it together!" Bear said.
He lifted up Badger, who lifted up
Mole, who lifted up Hedgehog,
who lifted up Mouse.
   "I can't believe I'm doing this!"
Badger grumbled as they
wobbled and swayed.

Mouse stretched up high and
tied the star to the tallest branch.
 "Oooh!" she gasped, watching
it sparkle.
 "Ahhh!" sighed Mole in
wonder.

"Eeek!" Badger giggled. "Mole, your feet are so tickly!"

"I can't help it!" chuckled Mole as they teetered and tottered.

And with a BUMP! they all fell to the ground.

Bear scrambled up. "Everything's perfect!" he said. "Now let's all wait for Santa."

So the friends huddled together as darkness fell.

"It's very cloudy," Hedgehog said. "What if Santa doesn't spot our tree?"

"He'll see it," Bear said with a smile.

But the time passed slowly and the wind began to whistle.

"I'm cold," Mole shivered. "I want to go home."

"Time for hot cocoa!" said Hedgehog, snuggling close.

But there was still no sign of Santa.

"He's not coming, is he?" cried Hedgehog.

"No presents?" sighed Mouse.

"Maybe Santa *isn't* coming after all . . ." thought Bear.

Suddenly, a big gust of wind blew the
clouds away. The moon shone down on the Christmas
star, making it shimmer and sparkle.

"There's something in the sky," Badger said.

"It's . . . it's . . ."

"SANTA!" Mouse cried out.
"And he's got presents!
HOORAY!"

"Ho! Ho! Ho!" laughed Santa. "I could see that
shiny star from way up high!"
There was a special gift for each of the friends.
"Thank you, Santa!" they said.
"No – thank *you!*" chuckled Santa.
"A rest and some yummy snacks were
just what my tired reindeer needed."
"It's thanks to Bear," Badger said.
"He always knew you'd come!"

"What a wonderful welcome this is,"
said Santa, shaking Bear by the paw.
"A clever bear like you could help me
deliver these presents. Tell me, will
you come along?"

"Yes! Yes! YES!" Bear exclaimed. He hopped
into the sleigh and his friends all cheered.
And as they flew off into the night sky,
Bear and Santa called out together:

"Merry Christmas, everyone . . .
and NEVER stop believing!"

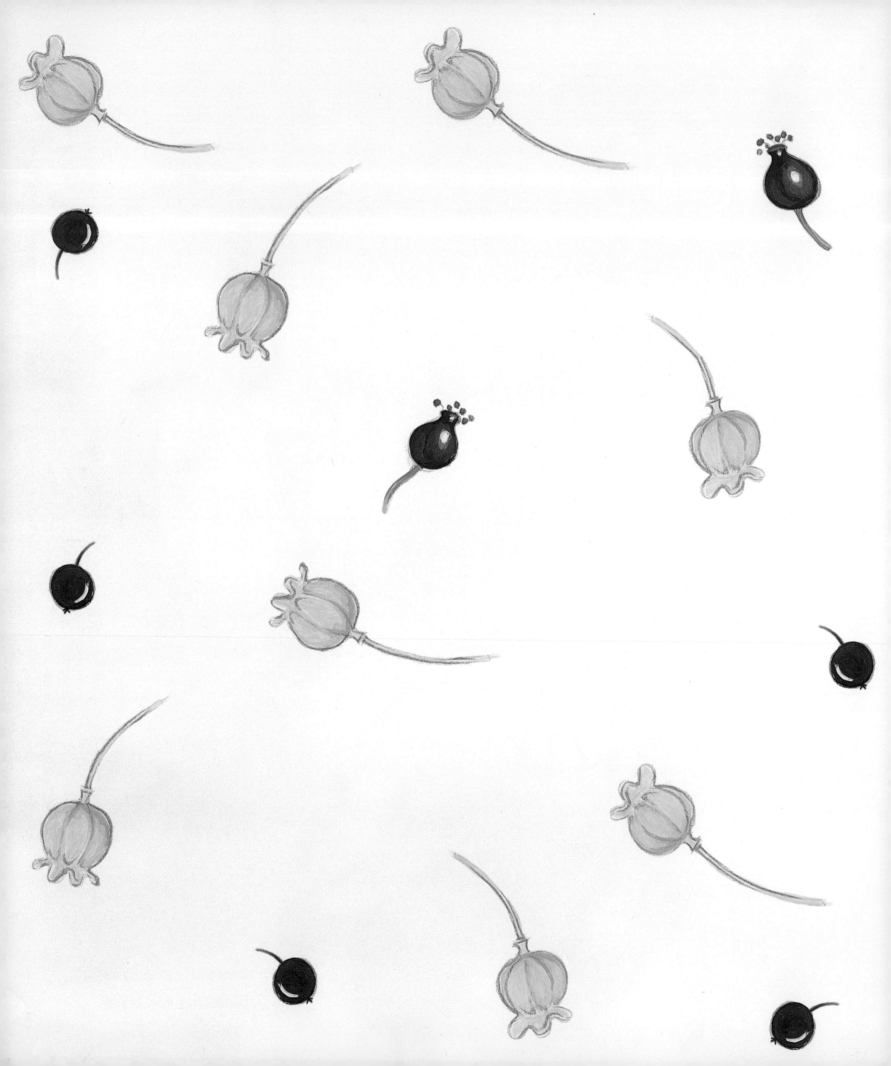

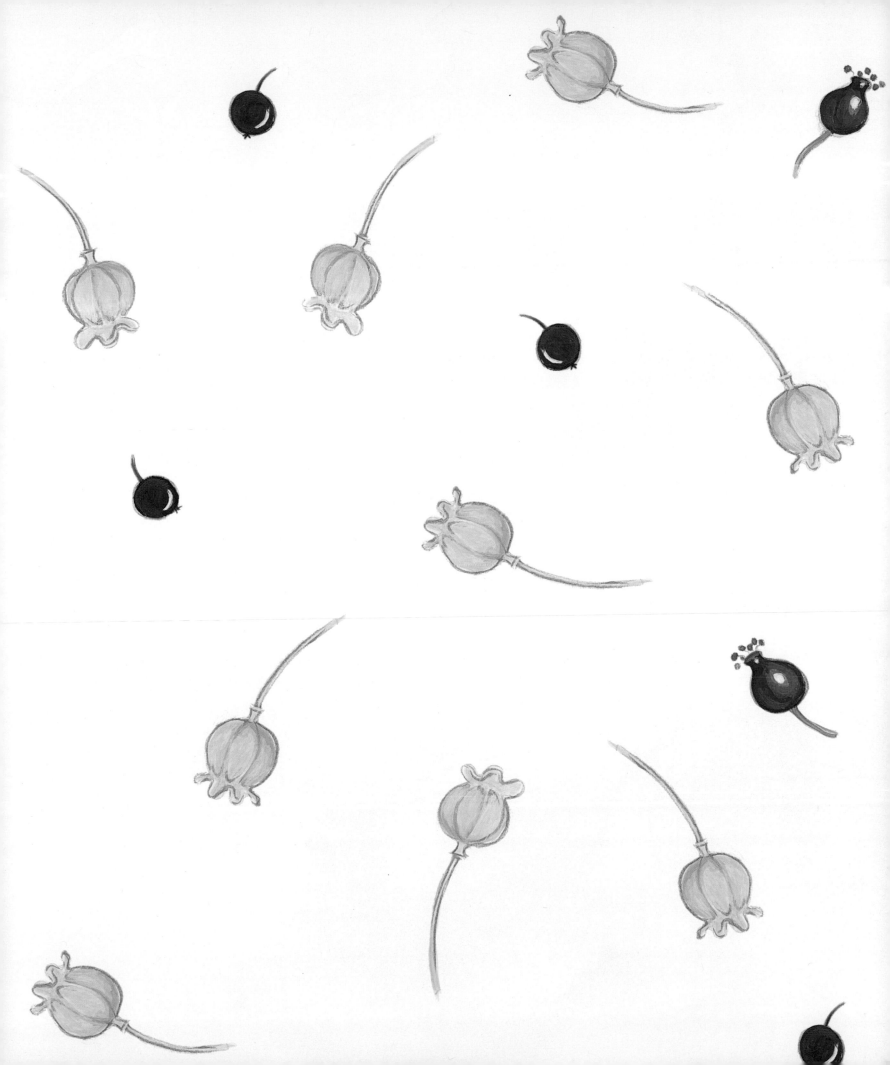

More stories to cherish at Christmas...

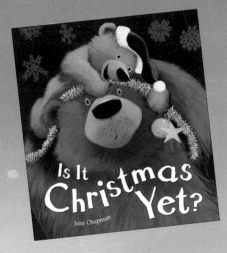

Is It Christmas Yet?

Jane Chapman

The Night Before Christmas

Clement C. Moore · Mark Marshall

Puppy's First Christmas

A Soft-to-Stroke Book

Steve Smallman · Alison Edgson

THE MAGICAL SNOW GARDEN

Tracey Corderoy · Jane Chapman

When Granny SAVED Christmas

JULIA HUBERY · CAROLINE PEDLER

Grumpy Badger's Christmas

Paul Bright · Jane Chapman

For information regarding any of the above titles or
for our catalogue, please contact us:
Little Tiger Press, 1 The Coda Centre,
189 Munster Road, London SW6 6AW
Tel: 020 7385 6333
E-mail: contact@littletiger.co.uk · www.littletiger.co.uk